MAXi GOES FOR THE GOLD

WRITTEN BY AARON MENDELSOHN
ILLUSTRATED BY TODD DAKINS

One of Four Stories
in The Adventures of Taxi Dog Series

Text by Aaron Mendelsohn • Illustrations by Todd Dakins

Book design by Noble Pursuits LLC with art direction by Elaine Noble

www.maxigoesforthegold.com • www.peekaboopublishing.com

See-Saw Publishing
Part of the Peek-A-Boo Publishing Group

FIrst Edition 2017 • Printed by Shenzhen TianHong Printing Co., Ltd. in Shenzhen, China

ISBN: 978-1-943154-83-8 (Hardback)
ISBN: 978-1-943154-84-5 (Paperback)

10 9 8 7 6 5 4 3 2 1

"Break time, Maxi, we'll wait here in the shade," says Jim.
"Arf, arf!"
"Oh, you want to play some tricks with your ball?"

"Okay, you toss,
I'll catch with my left hand."

"Okay, now my right hand."

"Now guess which hand is behind my back."

"Pretend we're training for obedience trials."
"Speak."
"Woof."

"Scaredog."

"Sleepydog."

"Someday we'll make the doggie Olympics."

A twelve-year-old boy interrupts them, climbing into the back seat.

"Hey mister, are you the driver of this cab?"

"Yes, I'm Jim, and this is Maxi."

"I'm Adam and I just moved to New York.
I've never taken a taxi before, but I need to get to my new gymnastics class."

"Just tell me where you want to go, and we'll get you there," replies Jim.

Adam said, "Okay, that's easy. Take me to the
Westside Gymnastics Center on Columbus Avenue"

"OK, buckle up," says Jim.

"This is my first day. I'm a little nervous. What if my new coach is too strict?" asks Adam.

"You know, I get nervous when I try something new too.
The first time I met Maxi I was nervous about taking care of a dog."

"Woof"

"But we believed there was nothing to be scared of and you know what?
It worked out great. We are best friends. Right, Maxi?"

"Rruff"

"Your destination, good sir," says Jim.
"That'll be eight dollars for the trip."

"Who do you think you are, Tarzan of the rings?"
asks Adam laughing.

"Arf."

Maxi jumps up to reach the high bar.

"You can't do that alone Maxi, and you need chalk on your paws."

Maxi flops across the bar. "Woof, woof."

"Okay, show-off, my turn."

Maxi jumps onto the pommel horse
and overshoots it.

"Are you okay?" asked Adam.

"Arf."

Maxi goes to the balance beam to climb on.

"Hello!" is suddently heard
from an unseen doorway

"Oh, Oh!" said Adam
"We are in trouble now."

"I'm Sonja, your coach.
I see you've been trying out the equipment."

"Hi! I'm Adam and this is Maxi,"
Adam says nervously.

"Well, Maxi, we don't usually allow dogs in the gymnastics center, but you remind me of my dog named Gorgeous who became a great performer.

"Don't be nervous, Adam. You're not in trouble. This class is all about having fun while learning the proper skills," said Sonja.

Adam and Maxi breathe sighs of relief.

"Let's get some chalk on our hands first for grip."

"Woof."

"Maxi wants to try the balance beam," said Adam.
"Ladies and Gentlemen, on the beam, from
New York City, Maxi The Taxi Dog."

Maxi tries and falls off.

Maxi tries again and makes it.

"You want to try, Adam?" asks Sonja.

A nervous Adam manages to stay on and then jumps off and sticks the landing. He raises his arms in triumph.

"Nice work!" exclaims Sonja.

"Thanks for showing me there's nothing to be scared of Maxi. I'm not nervous anymore."

"Woof."

Sonia comes out to the cab
to commend Maxi. "Hi! I'm Sonja."

"Hi! I'm Jim."

"Your dog has great potential.
Maxi's performance on the
balance beam was incredible."

"Arf."

"Both of you are welcome back anytime."

"Bye, Maxi," says Adam. "You were a great help. Bye Jim."

As Jim's cab drives off down the street,
Maxi's howl trails behind it.

"Doggie Olympics here we come!"

The End